IT'S NOT ABOUT THE PUMPKIN!

Veronika Martenova Charles

Illustrated by David Parkins

TUNDRA BOOKS

Published in Canada by Tundra Books,
75 Sherbourne Street, Toronto, Ontario M5A 2P9

Published in the United States by Tundra Books of Northern New York,
P.O. Box 1030, Plattsburgh, New York 12901

Library of Congress Control Number: 2009938445

Library and Archives Canada Cataloguing in Publication

Charles, Veronika Martenova
    It's not about the pumpkin! / Veronika Martenova
Charles ; illustrated by David Parkins.

(Easy-to-read wonder tales)
ISBN 978-0-88776-949-8

    1. Fairy tales. 2. Children's stories, Canadian (English).
I. Parkins, David II. Title. III. Series: Charles, Veronika
Martenova. Easy-to-read wonder tales.

PS8555.H42242I877 2010   jC813'.54   C2009-905861-8

We acknowledge the financial support of the Government of Canada through
the Book Publishing Industry Development Program (BPIDP) and that of the
Government of Ontario through the Ontario Media Development Corporation's
Ontario Book Initiative. We further acknowledge the support of the Canada Council
for the Arts and the Ontario Arts Council for our publishing program.

ONTARIO ARTS COUNCIL
CONSEIL DES ARTS DE L'ONTARIO

Printed and bound in Canada

1 2 3 4 5 6   15 14 13 12 11 10

CONTENTS

THE PUMPKIN
PART 1

On Monday afternoon

Lily and Ben went to Jake's house.

"What are you doing?"

asked Lily.

"I have to make a picture

for school," said Jake.

"We're working on

the *Cinderella* story."

"What will you draw?" asked Ben.

"I don't know yet," Jake answered.

"You could draw Cinderella

in her pretty dress," said Lily.

"No way! That's boring.

I think I'll draw

a giant pumpkin," Jake said.

"There is no pumpkin

in *Cinderella*," Lily told him.

"There is so," said Jake.

"The fairy godmother

gives it to Cinderella,

and she goes to the ball in it."

"No, she doesn't," said Lily.

"My mom read *Cinderella* to me,

and that's not how it goes."

"Then how does it go?" asked Jake.

"Cinderella's coach

comes out of a hazel tree,"

Lily answered.

"What's a hazel tree?" asked Ben.

"It's a nut tree," said Lily.

"Listen! I'll tell you

the story I know."

ASH GIRL

(*Cinderella* from Europe)

Once there was a rich man

who had a wife and a daughter.

One winter, when snow

covered the ground, the wife

got sick and died. A year later,

the father married a widow

with two daughters.

They were beautiful,

but evil in their hearts.

They took away his daughter's
pretty dresses and made her
their kitchen maid.

She did all the work and slept
on the dusty kitchen floor.

They called her Ash Girl.

Every day, Ash Girl went

to her mother's grave and wept.

She planted a branch there

and her tears watered it. It grew

into a hazel tree. A white bird

made the tree its home.

One day, the king announced
there would be a masked ball
that was to last for three nights.
"What shall we wear, Mother?"
The two daughters talked
about dresses all day.

When her father suggested

that Ash Girl should have

a dress too, the sisters said,

"What? Is Ash Girl going with us?

Just look at how dirty she is!

She would disgrace us all."

So the father said nothing.

The night of the ball, Ash Girl

helped her sisters dress

and watched her family drive off.

She went to her mother's grave.

"Oh, I wish I could go," she sighed.

The bird on the tree sang,

"Shake the tree, shake the tree,

open the first nut that you see."

Ash Girl shook the tree

and opened the nut that fell.

A golden dress and shoes were inside.

After she had dressed herself,

the hazel tree opened, and from it

came a coach with horses.

As Ash Girl rode away,

the white bird called:

"Be home before midnight!"

When Ash Girl entered the palace,

everyone looked at her in wonder.

The king danced only with her.

As midnight neared, Ash Girl

remembered the bird's warning.

She slipped away and rode home.

The next day, the sisters spoke

of nothing but the lovely dancer

and her beautiful dress.

"Don't you wish you'd been there?"

they teased Ash Girl.

The next night was like the first.

But on the third night,

Ash Girl forgot to watch the time.

When the clock struck midnight,

she hurried away

and lost a shoe on the steps.

The king picked it up,

and the next day he started

to look for its owner.

"Whoever the shoe fits," he said,

"will become my queen."

When he arrived at the house

of Ash Girl's father, he asked

the girls who lived there

to try on the shoe.

The eldest daughter tried

the shoe on in her room.

It was too small.

"Cut off your toe!" her mother said,

"Once you're the queen,

you'll never have to walk again."

The daughter cut off her toe,

squeezed her foot into the shoe,

and went to show the king.

The king took her to the palace.

As they rode by the graveyard,

the bird on the hazel tree sang,

"Look at the blood on her shoe,

she is not the bride for you."

The king took the girl

back to her home.

Then he asked the mother,

"Do you have another daughter?"

The second sister tried the shoe,

but her foot was too big.

She cut her toe off too,

but again, the bird sang,

and again, the king returned her.

"Have you any other daughters?"

the king asked.

"Just one more!" the father said.

"But that shoe can't be hers!"

the stepsisters cried.

"Bring her here," said the king.

Ash Girl was brought in,

and the shoe fit perfectly.

So, Ash Girl became the queen.

The sisters limped to the wedding,

and they had to limp

for the rest of their lives.

★ ★ ★

"You know what?" said Ben,

"I know another *Cinderella* story.

It doesn't have

a pumpkin in it, either."

"Tell us your story," said Jake.

"Okay. It goes like this."

★

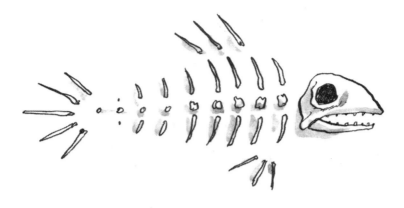

FISH BONES

(*Cinderella* from China)

Once, there was a girl called Lin.

When her mother died,

Lin's father married again.

The new wife also had a daughter.

A while later, the father died.

Lin was left to live

with a stepmother who hated her

for being bright and gentle.

She sent Lin to dangerous places

to collect firewood

and fetch water from deep pools.

Once, Lin caught a tiny fish

with golden eyes.

She took it home with her

and put it in a bowl of water.

The fish grew very fast.

Soon it was so big that Lin

had to put the fish in a pond.

Every day she fed the fish

with bits of her own dinner.

The fish became her friend.

The stepsister spied on Lin

and saw her feeding the fish.

She went and told her mother

who said, "What?

Lin is playing with a fish,

instead of working?"

The next day,

the stepmother sent Lin

far away to collect wood.

"Leave your coat at home,

and I will patch the holes in it,"

the stepmother told her.

After Lin left, the woman

put on the girl's coat,

hid a sharp knife in the sleeve,

and went to the pond.

The fish thought Lin had come

with food and stuck its head out.

The stepmother killed the fish,

cooked it, and ate it.

It tasted much better

than an ordinary fish.

When Lin went

to feed her fish the next day,

it was not there.

Lin was very sad.

Suddenly, an old man

appeared in front of her.

"Don't cry," he told her.

"Your stepmother killed the fish,

but it still has magic powers.

Gather its bones and hide them.

Whenever you need something,

just ask the fish bones for it."

It was spring festival time.

The stepmother and her daughter

put on their finest clothes

to go to the feast.

"Can I come, too?" asked Lin.

"No!" said the stepmother.

"You must tend the garden."

After they left,

Lin asked the fish bones

for nice clothes to wear.

At once, she was dressed in a

feather gown and golden shoes.

"I will return everything,"

she promised, before she left.

Everyone stared when Lin

arrived at the festival,

"Who is that girl?" they asked.

The stepsister stared too,

and whispered to her mother,

"Look! Could that be Lin?"

Lin heard her and panicked.

She ran home so fast,

she lost her shoe on the way.

When the stepmother

and her daughter returned,

they saw Lin asleep in the garden.

They thought no more about it.

The following day,

a villager found the golden shoe,

and he sold it to the emperor.

The emperor admired the shoe

for its beauty and wondered,

Whose shoe is this?

He put the shoe on display

and asked all the women

in the land to come and try it.

But the shoe didn't fit anyone.

One night, Lin snuck away

to take the shoe

and return it to the fish bones.

The emperor's soldiers caught her
and brought her before him.
When the emperor saw her tiny feet
he said, "She must try the shoe."

Lin put it on. It fit perfectly,

and her rags changed

into the feather gown.

The emperor gazed at Lin,

and he fell in love.

He asked her to marry him.

The stepmother and stepsister

set off to see the wedding,

but on the way,

they were killed by falling rocks.

People buried them

in a grave of stones.

★ ★ ★

"Why is it always about a girl

who gets married

at the end?" asked Lily.

"I know a *boy Cinderella* story,"

said Jake.

"Do you want to hear it?"

"Tell us," Lily and Ben said.

★

THE BLACK COW

(*Cinderella* from India)

Anil lived with his parents

in a mountain village.

After his mother died,

his father married a woman

who had a daughter Anil's age.

Every day, Anil and his stepsister

took their cows to the forest.

In the evenings, the stepmother

would feed her daughter

fine cakes with meat,

but she gave Anil cakes of mud

with a bit of flour on top.

Anil didn't complain

because he was afraid of her.

But he was very hungry,

and as he walked in the forest

with the cows, he would cry.

One black cow noticed

and asked, "Why are you crying?"

At first Anil was surprised

that the cow could speak.

But then he told her about

the stepmother and his hunger.

"Don't cry," said the cow,

and she began to stamp

the ground with her hooves.

Fine sweets appeared,

and Anil quickly gathered them up.

He shared them with his stepsister,

but told her to keep it a secret.

Soon the stepmother noticed

that Anil was getting stronger.

He's drinking cow's milk,

she thought, and she grew angry.

She asked her daughter about it
and found out about the sweets
and the black cow. That evening,
the stepmother told her husband
that he must sell the cow.

Anil was sad

and went to tell the cow.

"Get on my back," said the cow.

"We will hide deep in the forest,

and I will take care of you."

Anil and the cow stayed

in the forest for a long time.

Near the place where they stayed

was a deep hole in the ground.

Inside, lived the Great Snake.

To honor him, every day the cow

poured her milk into the hole

for the snake to drink.

The Great Snake was pleased.

"Is it you who gives me the milk?"

The cow nodded her head.

"What can I give you in return?"

the Great Snake asked.

"I'd like you to dress my son

in a suit of gold," said the cow.

"I can grant that wish,"

said the Great Snake.

And instantly,

Anil was dressed in gold,

from his head to his toes.

One day as Anil bathed,

his shoe fell into the river.

A fish swallowed it.

A fisherman caught the fish

and sold it at the royal palace.

When the palace cook cut the fish,

the golden shoe fell out.

The princess came to see it.

"How beautiful," she sighed.

"I would like to meet the owner

of such a fine shoe."

Servants were sent out to find

the one who lost the golden shoe.

They looked up and down the river,

until they saw the shining boy

wearing only one shoe.

They took him to the palace

and brought him to the princess.

As soon as Anil saw her,

he forgot about the black cow.

In time, the two were married.

At their feast, Anil ate sweets

that tasted like the ones

the black cow used to feed him.

Suddenly, he remembered her

and rushed away to find her.

Anil found the cow in the forest.

He embraced her

and thanked her for everything.

Then he took her to the palace,

and they lived happily

with the princess for many years.

★ ★ ★

THE PUMPKIN
PART 2

"That was cute," said Lily.

"Anil married the princess.

But that story is not

like Cinderella."

"Yes it is," said Ben.

"Anil has a cruel stepmother

who treats him badly.

And he loses his shoe,

just like Cinderella."

"What are you doing?"

Lily asked Jake.

"I'm looking for green crayons.

I want to draw the Great Snake,"

said Jake.

"Me, too," said Lily and Ben.

And they did.

ABOUT THE STORIES

There are hundreds of *Cinderella* stories from different cultures around the world. These are three:

Ash Girl is based on *The Cinder Maid* by Joseph Jacobs, who reconstructed it from many versions told throughout Europe.

Fish Bones is from a Chinese tale called *Yeh-hsien*, one of the first *Cinderella* stories to be written down about a thousand years ago.

The Black Cow is one of the few boy *Cinderella* stories found, and it comes from India.

Do you know more *Cinderella* tales?